For Janet ~ G. L.   For Noah ~ T. W.

This format published by Scholastic Inc., 557 Broadway; New York, NY 10012
by arrangement with Little Tiger Press.
SCHOLASTIC and associated logos are trademarks
and/or registered trademarks of Scholastic Inc.
Scholastic Canada; Markham, Ontario
First published in the United States by Good Books, Intercourse, PA 17534
in 2006 as *Little Honey Bear and the Smiley Moon*

Original edition published in English by Little Tiger Press,
an imprint of Magi Publications, London, England, 2006.

Text copyright © Gillian Lobel 2006 • Illustrations copyright © Tim Warnes 2006

Honey Bear's Snowy Adventure

Gillian Lobel   Tim Warnes

Little Honey Bear couldn't sleep. Through his bedroom window the moon was shining as bright as day. The snowy woods glimmered in the brilliant moonlight. And surely the moon was smiling at him!

"Why, hello, Moon," cried Little
Bear. And he rushed out into
the glittering woods.

There in the moonlight was Lily Long Ears, making snow hares.

"Hello, Little Honey Bear," said Lily. "Couldn't you sleep either?"

"Oh Lily," said Little Bear, "the moon sailed right in front of my window, and she *smiled* at me!"

"Me too!" said Lily. "She's so big and smiley tonight. I just had to come out to say hello."

She showered Little Bear with snow. "Catch me if you can!" she cried, and darted away through the trees.

They ran through the moonlit woods into a wide snowy meadow. High above hung the moon and right across the frozen meadow ran a shining silver pathway.

"It's a pathway to the moon!" cried Little Bear. "Just think, Lily – we could walk all the way to the moon and say hello."

"Little Honey Bear," squeaked a tiny voice. "Can I come too?"

"'Course you can, Teeny Tiny Mouse," said Little Bear.

So off along the moonpath went the three friends.

"What shall we do when we get to the moon?" asked Lily.

"We shall have tea," said Little Bear, "and mooncakes and moonjuice!"

"What are mooncakes like, Little Honey Bear?" asked Tiny Mouse.

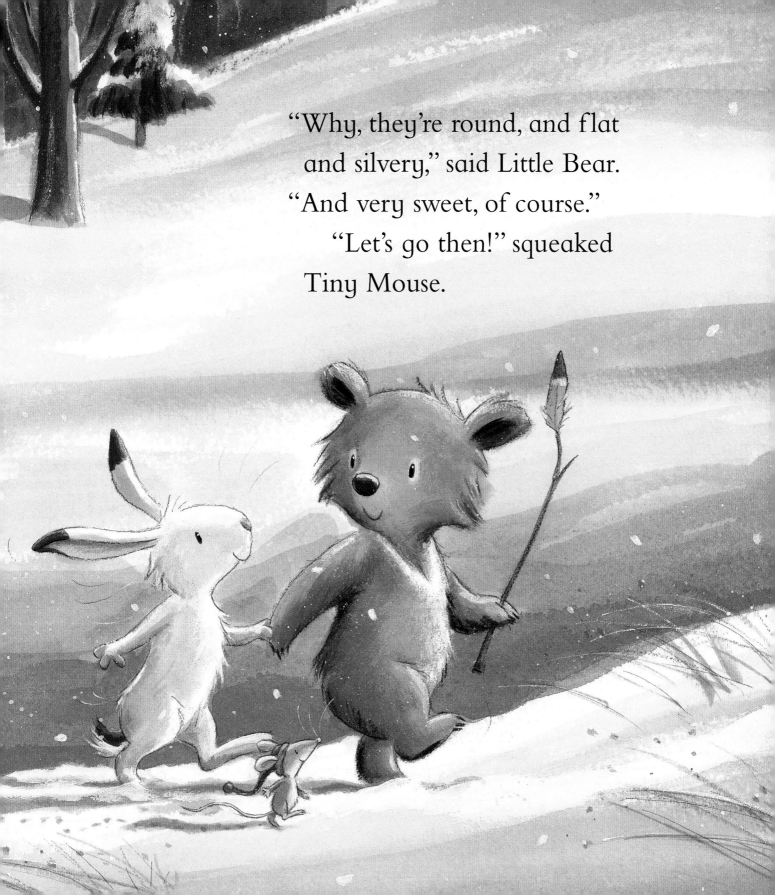

"Why, they're round, and flat and silvery," said Little Bear. "And very sweet, of course."

"Let's go then!" squeaked Tiny Mouse.

Suddenly the night grew colder.
A crisp wind whipped the snow
into little flurries. The path
to the moon grew steeper and
steeper.

"It's an awfully long way to
the moon," gasped Tiny Mouse.
"My little paws are freezing."

So Little Bear scooped Tiny
Mouse into his paw and set him
on his big shoulder.

"That's much better!" said
Tiny Mouse, tucking his toes
into Little Bear's thick furry coat.
"My paws are happy now."

Up and up ran the moonpath toward
the very top of the hill. Snowflakes stung
their eyes and whirled into their ears.

"Do you think we'll get there soon, Little Honey Bear?"
gasped Lily. "My ears are getting rather cold!"
As she spoke a great cloud blew in front of the moon . . .

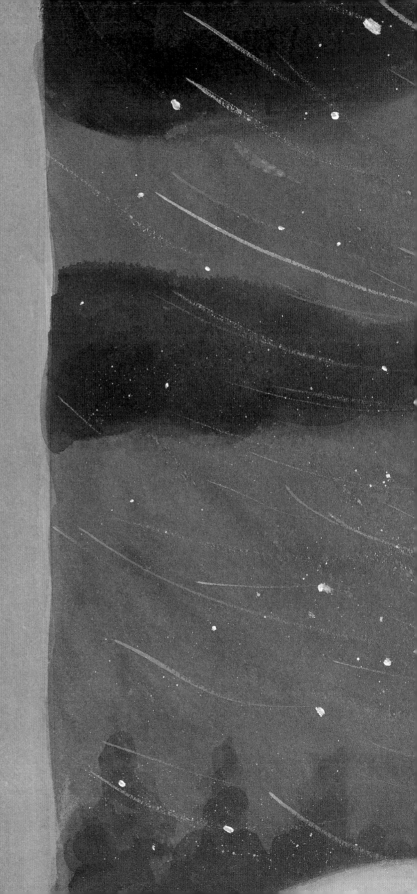

. . . and the moonpath
disappeared. Suddenly
it was very dark.

"I don't like it,
Little Honey Bear,"
said Lily. "I don't like
it at all!"

"I d-d-don't think
I want to go to the
moon after all," said
Tiny Mouse. "Even
for mooncakes."

So off they set
down the hill.

Down and down they slipped and slithered, until they reached the woods.

"Perhaps the moon is angry and doesn't want to see us after all," said Little Honey Bear.

"I want to go home," quavered Tiny Mouse.

"Me too!" gasped Lily.

But everything looked
different in the dark,
and they couldn't find
their way home.

The trees creaked and
groaned, and the woods
were full of shadows.
  "I think we're lost,"
sniffed Little Bear. "And
I want my mommy!"

Suddenly a silvery light flooded the woods. And up above, bobbing between the trees, the smiling moon appeared.

"Hooray!" everyone cried. And then the moonlight fell upon a big furry bear, her arms open wide as she ran toward them.

"Oh Little Honey Bear, I'm so glad I've found you!" cried Mommy Bear. And she gave them all a very big bear hug.

"Oh Mommy," said Little Bear. "We were going to have tea with the moon, but then she got angry with us and hid."

"And we didn't get to drink moonjuice," sighed Tiny Mouse.

"Or taste mooncakes," said Lily sadly.

Mother Bear smiled as she took them all back to the warm bear house for a special moon supper, with golden honey cakes and warm milk to drink.

"The moon wasn't angry. She was there all along," she said. "Only the clouds were hiding her."

"Mommy," said Little Bear later,
as she tucked him up in his bed,
"I really did want to go and see
the moon."
"Why, Little Bear, we
don't need to go to the moon
to see her – she's all around us."

Little Honey Bear looked through
the window. Every tree was hung
with a thousand glassy rainbows in
the bright moonlight. And then the
moon sailed through the trees and
smiled at him.

"Goodnight, Moon," said Little
Bear, rubbing his eyes. Then he
turned over and fell fast asleep.